COME FLY
WITH
DEATH

Poems Inspired by the Artwork
of Zdzislaw Beksinski

WESLEY D. GRAY

DEDICATION

This book is dedicated to my loving wife, Brenda, and to our children, Elizabeth and Logan.

CONTENTS

ONE IN HELL

Bones wrapped in bones,
wrapped in layers,
layers of bone on bone;
encrusted earth of flesh
crumbles at our feet,
our feet formed of clay.
Your face, my face—
we melt into one.

Our place,
Our flesh,
Our bones,
heaped upon this pole,
this whipping pole,
this torture pole
jutting from the nightmare.

You give me hugs.
I taste your lips;
they are one inside my mouth
and fused in teeth,
blended as I bite,
and eat you whole
and eat your parts.

My heart still beats
somewhere inside your chest,
deep within your cage,
ribs stripped of flesh;
and your heart mingles, tickles,
tingles in my skull.

My eyes peel wide
to wicked weather,
creeping fog,
settling dew
saturated with our fluids;
rain of skin
falls softly now upon us.

Me, you, we—
there is no start,
there is no end;
our twisted corpses
stretching on
forever,
and forever—
we are intertwined.

DEAD SWEET LOVE

Love in my arms—
my lover's corpse;
her skull rests
in my own dead hands.
She decomposes so sweetly;
I taste her death.
Her soul is cold.
Rotting legs around my waist—
I wear her like a shroud.
She melts into my lap.
My open spine tingles
as she withers
and lays her kisses upon my neck.

OCEAN EYES

Beneath the crescent moon
I'll know your scent,
buried in the breeze that sweeps your hair.
I'll taste you on the shore,
salted skin sweet with sweat,
flesh made orange upon the grit.
I'll swim inside your ocean eyes,
pulled so hard within your tides,
and drown inside your depths.

NIGHTMARE DREAMER

The Nightmare Dreamer
melts into the stone
as desperate bone
grovels at his feet.

Fused into the mold
of lost temples,
a shroud of flesh
wrinkles across his lap.

He envisions beauty,
yet his dreams are Death
manifested from a Hell
breathing beneath his cap.

Your fears are his to keep,
walking plainly among the earth.
His dream becomes your reality—
as he forever sleeps.

HELL FOSSIL

Men of lost goals
and minuscule purpose
lie crunched and broken,
impacted with the weight

of hollow burden,
angered with the memories,
to bleed forever
with their brethren.

Armies pile high in cold-stone fusion.
They died amidst the pit.
They brought their war to Hell
and marched upon the Black Gates.

Their skulls still don the helmets
of their killing suits,
their death rags,
their funeral wrappings.

Their spines drip upon on the wall,
crags layered with the corpses—
a bluff of rot and suffering
erodes softly into the abyss.

BRING THE LIGHT

What wretched creatures lie before me!
Squealing, squirming in the dark,
enthralled
amidst their feasting orgy.

Gnashing teeth, spattering blood,
festering bone;
their tongues dance along the drips
of other men's pain.

A cryptic overseer
looms beyond the mist,
his crow shoulders
pecking upon the scars.

A thousand wicked grins
gleam from rubble and from rot,
a pile of waste—
dead men leering in the dark.

A door to freedom is at their backs,
but most will never see it,
long since trading eyes
for sharper teeth and larger maws.

But I bring the Light,
and I wear the shroud.
My candle burns;
my flame never falters.

The Bearer of the Cross walks beside me.
We pass among the throng
and it parts before our steps;
like the splitting seas—

I bring the Light
and the darkness scatters.

DESOLATE PREY

Hands whisper in her mist;
finger ghosts
leaving but impressions of an echo—
tickling remnants of a relic touch.

Arachnid bones curl around her throat,
choking her down to faded breath.
Vertebrae tongue laps upon her breast,
tasting the haunt of a former self.

She is but flesh below the waist,
lustrous hips still curving with desire;
nothing more than bone above,
and rubbed so raw between.

Skeleton frames of men come and gone,
leaving her a wasteland, ravaged clean,
stripped like spoiled meat—
given fully to the vultures.

EARTHFACE

He wears the world on his face—
mountainous landscapes
merge to his façade;
screaming falls,
and bluffs of a lost valley
eclipsed upon his brow.
His cheeks bear marks of wind scar
trenched by screeching sands.
Rivers rip through flesh and bone;
bulging veins that scrape and branch,
twisting frames on a clay-formed skull.
His eye is the sun within its hole,
burning beneath his ravaged lid.
He'll not speak a word
of journey nor time
for his lips have fused
and his voice has slipped—
crumbling into erosion.

BONE TREE

There is a tree made of bone,
sprung from seeds of death,
with branches intertwined,
knobby joints and gnarled twists—
twigs chattering in the wind.

There is a tree made of bone
negating sprouts of life.
Once a sapling knuckle's mass,
now a skeletal complexity
rivals even stars.

There is a tree made of bone
standing opposite to life,
growing contrast to the flourishing
never to know blooming,
or the tastes of a blossom scent.

There is a tree made of bone,
a counterpoint to life.
Down within its hardened shell
it breeds and churns the marrow,
osteoblastic breathing—
never dying,
stacking bone on bone.

You walk upon your winter,
of lost souls and fading light;
rooted deep within this hollow grove
there is a tree made of bone—
and it grows against your life.

FUTURE BOY

To us he is a foreigner,
yet the boy is hope upon the brim of the world,
born from death into a city that sleeps,
unto sadness,
and to a people who weep.

Our nightmare tongue will rear him
from a mold misplaced so long ago,
faded away like coherent thought,
forging the boy into a refuge
to stand indifferent to our rot.

He is a torch within our darkness.
The decayed night of our planet
will never make him bleed;
his hope lights and guides our path
into the days of futures unseen.

HOLD, CELESTIAL CHILD

Hold, child,
Precious life—
Mother's tears behind the shroud.

Child of the nighttime sky,
This is not your world;
You were born from the womb of stars.

Hold! Hold!
Grip the moon and hold!
Breathe the wind from Mother's breast;
Suckle at the tip of mountain's peak.

Hold, child!
Feel the sun inside your palm;
Taste the milk on ocean's lips.

Hold, child, and dream,
Dream of life.
Dream, and hold now—

For the Earth wanes,
And time will soon eclipse.

TRAVELER AT THE END OF THE WORLD

He walks the nightmare forest,
utopian sight against the dark.
His skies are a glamorous torch—
fires of the Sun running amok,
setting ablaze and kissing
a sweet-lit course to fading horizons.

Last of the guardians beneath his palm;
the beast will guide his path
through daunting trees
whose wisps give shade—
shadow children poised,
their fruit ripe for vengeance.

With bones set to crumble,
he walks the nightmare—
a journey to cross the world's edge;
but his eyes are with the ocean,
and he'll never see the end.

PIPER AT THE GATES OF HELL

I fret with skeleton fingers
a song to raise an army;
its tone will rattle the bones,
and tickle the ears of corpses,
summon Death's wing from a lost crypt,
to soar unchained above the forests.

I compose in drips and shadow.
My flute is made of marrow.
I play the remorse of madness,
sing lament unto the masses.

My tune has mind to steal a breath,
place urges into the dead.
My melody will snare the Reaper
its notes will bring him kneeling
to do my deeds and bidding.

SCAVENGER

Like a dog I crawl
throughout this treacherous wasteland—
yet I am a god among the cockroach masses.

My mangled limbs
are only fit to scurry
along the dung heap and dirt.

I no longer see the city that burns,
for blood and cobwebs mask my face.
But I need not see to know it burns.

I hear the distant crackles,
intertwined with cackles,
and all those hovering screams.

I sense a tormented heat
and breathe the charring scent
of their flesh throughout the night.

DEATHFUSION

To become one with your lover
is an affair that stands beyond all time—
to feel her melt within you
as you leave one world for the next.

Taste her lips inside your throat,
as your heart beats
a sweet-laced cadence
against her dying breast.

Her thighs ooze into your lap;
liquid pool of her seduction
solidified
to blissful warmth upon your groin.

Your eyes blend
within her graying matter,
a vision now peering
far beyond her skull.

She breathes inside you—touch her, taste her,
know her now as you never could.
Love her as she joins your flesh,
and you shall never come apart.

COME FLY WITH DEATH

Come fly with Death
and feel the splitting as you come apart
with turbulent screams bifurcating bones.

Flee further from this life—
unfurl your wings and soar
with tangled feathers cutting the night.

Join his skeleton beak,
slicing stabs at airless wind,
and wield its dashing spine.

Stay near to glinting shroud and glide,
knowing tattered wings will guide,
as whispering scars are left behind.

Go now into that hollow abyss,
but do not pass the dark in calmness;
break the barrier with raging clamor!

Do not scrape or merely crawl.
Come fly with Death—
and swoop, and yawp, and bawl.

CORPSE-HEAD BRIDE

Trading her body for a dress,
the silken white gown
shrouds away her loss.

Mirror worlds grimace at her back,
bursting with fantasies
she'll never enter alone.

Blood-stained desert surrounds her,
separates her from her groom.
Her frozen eyes are trenched in longing;
her ghost face bleeds like snow.

Oceans and dreams bloom behind her,
blossoming out in fruitless hope.
She wonders and she waits—
gazing forward,
into a starless horizon.

BORN UNTO THE CRYPT

Rock-a-bye Baby down in the pit,
blue-shrouded ghost
sings a sultry lullaby.

Skeleton hands tickle at the flesh,
with a rattle of bones to occupy
the newborn's time for just a while.

Baby yawns and gives a stretch,
all tucked in for slumber.
Playmates wither upon the wall,
while rotting crows feast upon the dead.

Sway, Baby, sway.
Drift to sleep and dream.
Dream of darkened skies,
ominous, churning eyes.

Dream of distant wishes,
rags to riches,
and all those horrors kept
by chains, and hooks,
in death.

CRUCIFIED REMAINS

With arms outstretched
I pray to a lost sun,
listening to the splitting of my skin,
for these are all the screams
I have left to surrender.

No longer do I bleed,
yet the nails never end
in pinning me to suffering.

My fingers curl,
cringing at the pain,
as tormentors mock me,
haunt me,
taunt me from their distant clouds.

The spectral faces
of my own madness
play the only witness,
as torrid wind tickles
the litters that remain
of my tattered flesh.

REVERSE REGURGITATION

They clamor to the mouth
in reverse regurgitation,
spilling beyond the teeth
to slide down his withered tongue.

Like spiders they crawl,
the tempestuous mob,
tortured souls within mangled bodies,
piles of fetid corpses,
insects husks all dried and brittle,
fused and rotting.

They struggle to get ahead,
desperate to end the madness.
They battle against their brethren
to be first in line,
to claim the right,
for Death's head to consume them.

ACKNOWLEDGEMENTS

First Publication Credits:

- "Earthface." *Indigo Rising Magazine*, June, 2011.
- "One in Hell." *Dark Gothic Resurrected Magazine*. October, 2011.
- "Ocean Eyes." *Dark Gothic Resurrected Magazine*. October, 2011.
- "Dead Sweet Love." *Dark Gothic Resurrected Magazine*. October, 2011.
- "Desolate Prey." *Twisted Dreams Magazine*. October, 2011.
- "Traveler at the End of the World." *Twisted Dreams Magazine*. October, 2011.
- "Hold, Celestial Child." *Twisted Dreams Magazine*. October, 2011.
- "Hell Fossil." *Death Head Grin Anthology Vol. 2*. April, 2012.
- "Piper at the Gates of Hell." *The Horror Zine*. August-September Issue, August, 2012.
- "Future Boy." *The Horror Zine*. August-September Issue, August, 2012.
- "Bring the Light." *The Horror Zine*. August-September Issue, August, 2012.
- "Come Fly with Death." *Fossil Lake: An Anthology of the Aberrant*. Sabledrake Enterprises, April, 2014.

Reprinted Publication Credits:

- "One in Hell." *Gothic Poems and Fiction*. Static Movement, August, 2013.
- "Ocean Eyes." *Gothic Poems and Fiction*. Static Movement, August, 2013.
- "Dead Sweet Love." *Gothic Poems and Fiction*. Static Movement, August, 2013.

- "Piper at the Gates of Hell." *The Horror Zine Digest.* Summer 2012 (Volume 1). October, 2012.
- "Future Boy." *The Horror Zine Digest.* Summer 2012 (Volume 1). October, 2012.
- "Bring the Light." *The Horror Zine Digest.* Summer 2012 (Volume 1). October, 2012.

Cover Image:

Copyright: Elena Schweitzer (Shutterstock.com).

ABOUT THE AUTHOR

Wesley D. Gray is a writer, an author of fiction, and a self-proclaimed poet. He writes about those things that interest him most, primarily within the realm of speculative fiction, but under the name of Rafe Grayson, he finds an outlet for channeling his darkest horrors.

Crafting his words with a flair for the twisted, the beautiful, and the strange, he writes because he has to, because he enjoys it, because it is his passion.

When he isn't working, Wesley enjoys typical nerdy activities like reading, playing video games, and tabletop gaming with family and friends. He resides in Florida with his wife and two children.

If you're ready to delve deeper, be sure to visit his blog, Marrowroot.com.

Also connect via:
- WesDGray.com
- Twitter: @wesdgray
- Facebook.com/wesleydgray.writer
- Amazon.com/author/wesleygray
- Google.com/+WesleyDGrayWriter
- Goodreads.com/wesleydgray

CPSIA information can be obtained
at www.ICGtesting.com
Printed in the USA
LVOW10s1753041216
515762LV00001B/18/P

9 780692 288894